RIKI LEVINSON

Watch the Stars Come Out

ILLUSTRATED BY DIANE GOODE

E. P. DUTTON   NEW YORK

Text copyright © 1985 by Riki Friedberg Levinson
Illustrations copyright © 1985 by Diane Goode

Library of Congress Cataloging in Publication Data
Levinson, Riki.   Watch the stars come out.
Summary: Grandma tells about her mama's journey
to America by boat, years ago.
1. Children's stories, American.   [1. United States—
Emigration and immigration.   2. Grandmothers—Fiction]
I. Goode, Diane, ill.   II. Title.
PZ7.L5796Wat   1985   [E]   84-28672
ISBN 0-525-44205-7

Published in the United States by E. P. Dutton,
2 Park Avenue, New York, N.Y. 10016

Published simultaneously in Canada by
Fitzhenry & Whiteside Limited, Toronto

Editor: Ann Durell   Designer: Riki Levinson

for my Mort and Gerry—
remembering Anna, my Mama
R.L.

to Peter Goode
D.G.

Grandma told me when her Mama was a little
girl she had red hair—just like me.

Grandma's Mama loved to go to bed early and
watch the stars come out—just like me.

Every Friday night, after the dishes were put
away, Grandma's Mama would come to her room
and tell her a special story.

When I was a little girl, my big Brother and I went on a big boat to America. Mama and Papa and Sister were waiting there for us.

My aunt, Mama's sister, took us to the boat. She didn't bring my two little brothers. They were too small. They would come on a boat when they were older.

Aunt gave us a barrel full of dried fruit. She asked an old lady to watch over us. And she did. She also ate our dried fruit.

The old lady and Brother and I went down the steps to our room. I counted the steps as we carried our bundles down, but there were so many, I forgot to count after a while.

Sometimes the boat rocked back and forth—it was fun! Some people didn't like it—they got sick. The old lady got very, very sick. She died.

Brother told me not to worry. He would take care of me—he was ten.

At night when I went to sleep, I couldn't see
the stars come out in the sky. That made me sad.

Each morning when we got up, Brother put a mark on his stick. I counted them—twenty-three.

The last morning we looked across the water. There were two islands near each other. One of them had a statue standing on it—a lady with a crown. Everyone got very excited and waved to her. I did too.

When the boat stopped, we carried our
bundles down the plank.

I started to cry. I did not see Mama and Papa
and Sister. A sailor told me not to worry—we
would see them soon.

We went on another boat to a place on an
island.

We carried our bundles into a big, big room.
Brother and I went into a small room with all
the other children without mamas and papas.
A lady looked at me all over. I wondered why.
I waited for Brother. The lady looked at him too.

The next day we went on a ferry. The land came closer and closer as we watched. Everyone waved. We did too.

Mama and Papa and Sister were there!

We went on a trolley to our home. Mama said
it was a palace.

Mama's palace was on the top floor. I counted
the steps as we walked up—fifty-two!

Mama and Papa's room was in the middle. Our room was in the front. And in the back was the kitchen with a big black stove.

Mama warmed a big pot of water on the stove. She poured some into the sink and helped me climb in to wash.

Mama washed my hair, and when it was dry,
she brushed it. It felt good.
Sister gave us cookies and glasses of tea.
I was very tired.

I kissed Mama and Sister good-night. Papa patted me on my head and said I was his little princess.

I went into our room and climbed into Sister's bed. It was right next to the window.

I watched the stars come out. One, two, three.

This Friday night I will go to bed very early
and watch the stars come out in the sky.
I hope Grandma will come to my room and
tell me another special story.

Behind the Scenes

Fun-To-Do Activities Begin on Page 50

Behind the Scenes

Introduction

Watch the Stars Come Out is about a young girl who tells the story of her Great Grandma's journey to the United States. Her great grandmother left the country where she was born and arrived in another country, to make that her new home. A person who moves into a foreign country to live is called an *immigrant*. This is a story about immigrants. It is a story of one special family's history.

New Beginnings

Immigrants came to the United States for many reasons. People travelled a long way because they felt America might hold the promise of a better life for themselves and for their families. Other people came to practice their religion freely. And others because they wanted to leave countries where they saw poor people around them starving. Between 1815 and 1915, 30 million people from France, Italy, Russia, Spain, Poland, Hungary, Greece and other countries emigrated to America. *Emigrate* means leaving one country to settle in another. Today the United States is a nation of people who have emigrated. It is a place where people from all types of backgrounds and cultures live together.

The early immigrants arriving in America came by ship, docking at Ellis Island in the New York harbor. Each person was examined by a doctor. They were given a list of questions to answer. Some immigrants who had very difficult names were given new ones that were easier to say and spell. You may know someone who changed their name. Trace your last name. You may find out that it wasn't the same one that your relatives had many years ago!

Ellis Island

Pilgrims Were Immigrants

The Pilgrims were the first immigrants to come to America. In 1620, they left England because the Church would not allow them the freedom of prayer. They set out to cross the Atlantic. During a storm, their ship was unexpectedly tossed into Plymouth Harbor, on the coast of Massachusetts. Here the Pilgrims found a home.

Behind the Scenes

The first winter was difficult for the Pilgrims. Many of them starved. Then a friendly Indian named Squanto taught the new settlers how to plant corn, how to hunt, and how to fish. By the summer, the colony was a success. There was enough food for everyone and even some left over to store for the coming winter.

In September, the Pilgrims harvested their crops. They prepared a big feast and invited 91 Indians. The Pilgrims gave thanks for being alive, for having plenty to eat, and for being in a new land.

Today, we share the Pilgrims' early feelings of gratitude by setting aside a day to remember these settlers. We call this day Thanksgiving Day—a custom started by immigrants more than 350 years ago.

Immigrants Today

Living in America continues to be a dream for many people. Everyday more immigrants come into the United States and decide to make it their new home.

Before 1965, most immigrants came from Europe. But today's immigrants come from Asia, Latin America and the Caribbean as well. Many

Cuban immigrants live in Florida. Their community adds a special Spanish flavor to the city. In the West, especially in California, Filipinos live and work. They left the Philippine Islands because of poverty and to find a better place to live. Today there are 800,000 Filipinos in America. In recent years, 400,000 Koreans have settled in New York and on the West coast. They emigrated from South Korea in order to find better education and more opportunities for their children.

These latest settlers have come to America for the same reasons that the earliest settlers arrived. And they have brought with them their own customs that now enrich American communities. Have you met anyone from another country? What did you find out about them?

Behind the Scenes

The American Family

There are so many different nationalities, races and religions that blend into the American culture, the United States is often called one big "melting pot." The United States population is made up of descendants of every part of the world. Here, there are more immigrants than in any other country in history. This mixture of languages, customs and traditions is valuable. And it gives America her cultural variety.

Immigrants You Know

Immigrants have helped make the United States the special country it is today. How many famous people in the list below do you know?

Famous Person	Place of Birth	Profession
Alexander Graham Bell	Scotland	inventor of the telephone
Albert Einstein	Germany	scientist
Arnold Schwarzenegger	Austria	actor and body builder
Martina Navratilova	Czechoslovakia	tennis star

Think of the many immigrants who became famous — movie and TV stars, and athletes too. After all, we are all immigrants — the only difference is *when* our families first landed on American shores.

Cultural Celebrations

People of all nationalities get to share the excitement of cultural celebrations brought to this country. Events and activities once unknown to the people of the United States are now observed every year. In which of the following have you taken part?

Mardi Gras

This event comes from an old French custom of parading an ox through the street. This reminded people not to eat meat for 40 days of Lent before Easter. The French who settled in New Orleans, where the biggest parade is now held, made this custom famous in the United States. Other cities hold festive carnivals, parades and masked costume parties.

Behind the Scenes

Chinese New Year

Gold paper dragons zigzag through the streets when people in Chinese communities around the world celebrate their New Year. It is not observed on January 1st because it is based on the ancient Chinese calendar. It comes each year in late January or early February and lasts for more than a week. Watch out for firecrackers, drums and excitement in the Chinatowns around the country when this holiday starts to stir.

St. Patrick's Day

This day is both a religious and national holiday reminder celebrated by the Irish. It is in honor to Ireland's green countryside, to Ireland's national flower, the green shamrock, and to Saint Patrick, the patron saint of Ireland. On March 17th, many children all over the country wear green—do you?

In New York City, more than 100 bands and 100,000 marchers parade through the streets. The event lasts four hours, and in four hours, you certainly see a lot of green. Some streets even get painted with green stripes to celebrate this special occasion.

Highland Games

At Grandfather Mountain in North Carolina, the contests, games and athletic events once held in the Highlands of Northern Scotland take place each year in July. Here, about 100 clans of Scotland meet to take part in traditional activities such as bagpiping competition, highland fling dancing, sheepherding exhibitions, and tossing the cabar. A *cabar* is a stripped pine tree with no bark or branches. Whoever can toss the cabar farthest into the air is the winner.

Pancake Day

The people of Olney, England, held the custom that when Lent began, they could not eat butter and eggs. So in order to use up these ingredients, they made pancakes the day before Lent. Today in Liberal, Kansas, people hold frying pans and line up to race—flipping the pancake in the pan three times before the finish line. They compare racing times with the people in Olney to see who is fastest.

Behind the Scenes

Proof In The Wearing

Part of who you are blends in with part of the people who are around you. Would it surprise you to know that we celebrate each other's differences by sharing them? For example many of the fabrics and styles in the clothes you wear are from other cultures.

Clothing	Country
beret	France
kilted skirt	Scotland
clogs	Sweden
sandals	Israel and Egypt
derby hat	England

Proof In The Pudding

Some foods brought to America by immigrants have become special favorites. Which one do you like?

Food	Country
hot dog	Germany
doughnut	The Netherlands
waffle	Belgium
chili	Mexico
pretzel	Germany

Being A Citizen

You are a citizen. Whatever country you were born in, you automatically become a citizen of that country. Citizens of a country have rights and privileges that others who are not citizens do not have. In the United States, a citizen has freedom of speech and of religion and the right to a free press. A citizen also has the right to elect the government. People's right to vote is a freedom, but it is also a responsibility — it is one way by which people protect their freedom and their rights as citizens.

How can you be a good citizen? You can take part in community activities. You can collect and recycle aluminum cans. You can put trash in proper containers. You can do volunteer work. By obeying the laws and by helping others around you, you take an active part in being a good citizen. Citizens' rights are contained in the United States Constitution. If you want to read a copy, check your local library.

September 17th is Citizenship Day. Think of how you can add a special touch to the next one. Celebrate your citizenship!

Behind the Scenes

If You Want To Be A Citizen

…you must:
- be at least 18 years old
- have lived in the U.S. for five years
- be able to read, write and speak English
- have a good record of obeying the law
- pass a test about the U.S.

Here are some questions that are on the test. Can you answer them?
- Who was the first President of the United States?
- How many states are there in the U.S.?
- Where is the Capitol of the U.S. located?

Each immigrant takes an oath to honor and be ready to defend his or her country.

American Symbols

A *symbol* is something that stands for something else. Symbols say something special about places, people and things. For example, a star on your homework assignment may be a symbol for your good work. A heart may be a symbol for love. There are familiar symbols that say something about our country too.

The Statue of Liberty stands for the liberty and freedom citizens in America have. The stars and stripes on the American flag stand for all the states of the United States and for the original 13 colonies. The bald eagle, which lives in the wild, reminds us of our freedom to also live as we wish.

Songs can be symbols. When "The Star Spangled Banner" is heard, Americans think of a country they can be proud of. Even the colors red, white and blue together remind us of the United States. Most of these symbols are known around the world. Other countries have their own symbols, like the shamrock and the color green of Ireland. And some countries share America's symbolic colors. Did you know that the French flag is red, white and blue, also?

Behind the Scenes

The Statue Of Liberty

"Look up!" all the immigrants said to one another as they approached America. Standing over 300 feet high, the Statue of Liberty was passed by millions of immigrants on their way to the New York harbor. When they saw her, they thought of the promise of freedom and opportunity in their new country.

The Statue of Liberty herself is an immigrant, given to the United States by the people of France and dedicated in 1886. The Statue of Liberty expresses the idea of liberty for all, an idea that both countries share. The proud figure holds a glowing torch. Her symbolic crown has seven spikes which stand for the seven continents and the seven seas. She carries a tablet with the date, July 4, 1776, the day America won independence. This date marks our liberty as a nation.

The statue was sculpted by a man named Frédéric Auguste Bartholdi. He used his mother as the statue's model. The tower inside was designed by Alexandre Gustave Eiffel, the man who designed the Eiffel Tower in Paris. Stairs and an elevator run through the 154-foot pedestal. From the crown, you can see a small part of our great land.

The Statue of Liberty's Interesting Sizes

The Statue of Liberty is so grand in size that just one fingernail is larger than this book! And her whole index finger is taller than two of you! The width of her mouth is the size of one yardstick. Take out a yardstick and see for yourself how big this is. How does the width of your mouth compare in size? The length of her nose is four feet six inches. Are you as tall as the Statue of Liberty's nose? Her right arm that holds the torch is 42 feet long. That's bigger than a two-story house! Look up more measurements — you will be even more surprised!

Star Light, Star Bright

In the story, *Watch the Stars Come Out,* the young girl sees a night sky full of brightness and shining stars. Just like her Great Grandma, she loves to gaze out the window. What do you suppose she saw in the stars?

In ancient times people watched the sky and imagined that the stars made up pictures. They made up stories about different groups of stars they saw there every night. A group of stars that forms a pattern is called a *constellation* (say: cahn-stuh-**lay**-shon). There are 88 constellations in the universe. Early farmers studied stars to know when to plant each season. Travelers have always watched the stars for directions. The North Star has guided ships and planes on long trips for many, many years. You can see the stars too on any clear night. What do you see in them?

Each star is enormous. One star is many times bigger than the earth — even though it looks much smaller. That's because it is so far away. Stars give off light. They can be red, blue, yellow, white or orange. Some twinkle, some do not. Watch the stars one night and see if you can find a flashing one.

Constellations You May Know

How many of these constellations do you know?

Milky Way
The best time to see this group of stars is in the summer. It is shaped like a giant pinwheel with most of the stars in the center. Long ago, people thought it was a weather cloud that looked milky. Others thought

it looked like a milk-white road. These theories might be how it got its name. What do you think?

Big Dipper

This group of seven stars can be found in the Northern sky. They are arranged in the form of a dipper. The Big Dipper is part of a larger group of stars called *Ursa Major*, or Great Bear.

Orion

These seven stars form the brightest constellation in the sky. Look for it in wintertime when it is brightest. People who saw Orion thought that its form looked like a hunter with a club in one hand and a shield in another.

At different times of the year, you can see different stars. It's fun to find pictures in the sky. One night you may see a rabbit, another night you may see a fish. The sky is a treasure. A place filled with a wealth of stories. Watch the stars and let your imagination go!

Activities ➡

Activities

Say Hello

Immigrants often greet one another in their native languages. Now you can try greeting friends in a different language, too.

Miss Liberty And Me

How do you measure up to the Statue of Liberty? It's easy to find out. All you need is a ruler and a friend to help you measure. Write your measurements on another piece of paper, then compare them to Miss Liberty.

Miss Liberty stands 151 feet 1 inch tall from her feet to the top of her torch.

- How tall are you?
- With your arm raised, how tall are you "from torch to toe?"

Miss Liberty's eyes are each 2½ feet wide.

- How wide are your eyes?

Miss Liberty's nose is 4½ feet long.

- How long is your nose?

Miss Liberty's hand is 16 feet long.

- How long is your hand?

One of Miss Liberty's fingers is 8 feet long.

- How long are your fingers?

Miss Liberty's arm is 42 feet long.

- How long is your arm?

Miss Liberty's mouth is 3 feet wide.

- How wide is your mouth?
- How wide is it when you're smiling?

Activities

Stargazing

When you look at a star-filled sky, search for different shapes. Many constellations of stars are named for the shapes they make. Read each riddle and guess the name of each constellation.

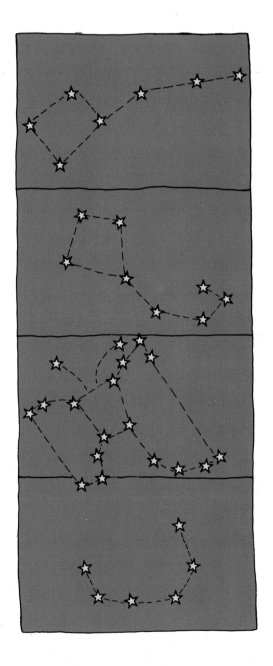

Some constellations are very big,
But I'm known for being little.
I've a bowl and a handle called a dipper
That will help you solve this riddle.

Something you fly
That rhymes with night,
Names this constellation —
A familiar sight.

Add what you spread on bread
To what planes can do
Will name this constellation
For me and for you.

You wear it on your head
And it rhymes with clown,
This constellation
Is called the Northern _____.

1. Little Dipper   2. Kite (also called Boötes)   3. Butterfly (also called Hercules)   4. Crown

Tasty Treat

We use the French word *hors d'oeuvre* (say: or-**derv**) to name party food served before the main meal. Here's an easy recipe for stuffed celery sticks. Treat your family with this hors d'oeuvre.

What You Need:
1   3-ounce package cream cheese, softened at room temperature
1   tablespoon milk
¼   cup raisins
¼   cup chopped walnuts
5   celery stalks, washed and cut into halves

What You Do:
- Blend the cream cheese with the milk, raisins and walnuts.
- Spread mixture on each piece of celery.
- Arrange the hors d'oeuvres on a dish. Serve before dinner.

Activities

This Is Your Life

Make a picture album of special happenings in your life.

What You Need:
a piece of light-colored construction paper, 8½ x 11 inches
tape, scissors and crayons

What You Do:
- Fold the construction paper in half the *long* way. Cut along the fold.
- Tape the two halves of paper together so you have one long piece.
- Fold the paper into 8 parts. (Hint: fold it in half, in half again, then in half once more—you'll have 8 equal sections.)
- Write your name and the day you were born on the first fold. Draw a picture of yourself there.
- On the remaining 7 folds, draw pictures of favorite events in your life. Write a few words about each event and the year it happened.
- Show your friends this story of your life.

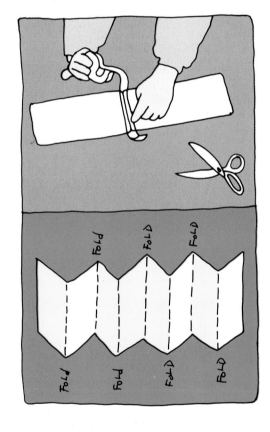

A Shopping Trip

Did you know that in America 200 years ago many people couldn't read? So shopkeepers painted pictures on their signs to describe their business. Can you name the shops pictured by these colonial signs?

If you had a shop, what would you sell? What would your sign look like?

Activities

Picture Messages

Today, pictures on signs give meaning to tourists travelling in countries where they don't speak the language. What do each of these signs (also called symbols) mean?

We've used these symbols to help tell a story, called a *rebus*. Can you "read" the pictures in the story?

Bobbi and Bob, identical twins, were happy that school was over for the day. Both of them were hungry, so they drove around until they found a (#1). Once inside, they decided to sit in the (#2) section. They both ordered burgers and salads—they were so hungry they hoped the service would be (#3), not (#4). After lunch, Bobbi and Bob hung out and talked about summer vacation. Bobbi really wanted to go (#5), but she had a job at the local (#7) every Saturday. After Bob and Bobbi paid for their food, they decided to (#6) home. They could tell vacation season was approaching, because there were lots of planes flying overhead, lifting off and landing at the nearby (#8).

Word Search

Hidden in the maze below are words you've just learned. Do you remember what they mean? The words go across and down. Find the words in the maze, then write them on another paper.

BUNDLE, CITIZEN, IMMIGRANT, ISLAND, LIBERTY, OCEAN, PILGRIM, STATUE, TRAVEL, STARS.

I	M	M	I	G	R	A	N	T	E
S	I	C	T	U	E	M	C	P	E
B	K	S	T	A	T	U	E	I	I
U	L	T	L	L	O	P	Y	L	S
N	B	A	X	O	C	R	C	G	L
D	T	R	A	V	E	L	W	R	A
L	W	S	Z	T	A	K	S	I	N
E	C	D	I	N	N	T	U	M	D
I	L	I	B	E	R	T	Y	O	U
C	I	T	I	Z	E	N	K	L	E

Activities

Pack Your Bags

Here's a word game that will stretch your imagination as far as it can go. You can play with others or by yourself. It's great when you are travelling in a car. To begin, pretend that you are moving to another country. What would you pack in your trunk? Name one item, then add a second item that begins with the last letter of the first item. Continue to add items until you run out of things to add. Remember: each item must begin with the letter of the last item added. For example: JEANS, SOCKS, SWEATER, RAINCOAT, and so on. You can play this game with two people or many more—it depends on how stuffed you want your trunk to be!

Can You Imagine That?

Are you bored by ordinary cars and planes and buses and trucks? Well, just close your eyes and imagine something new! Start with these unusual travel vehicles:

Wing-o-boat: a boat with an airplane wing
Propmobile: a car with a propeller
Pedal-bus: a schoolbus with pedals
Traincycle: a bicycle with a train wheel
Copteruck: a truck with a helicopter top

What color would a Wing-o-boat be? How many pedals would a Pedal-bus have? And how many drivers would it take to pedal the bus all the way to school? Why not get out a piece of paper and try drawing one of these?

Hide And Seek

When people made new homes in America they used lots of tools that are hiding in this picture. Can you find a hammer, a saw, a wrench, a ladder, a pail and a paint brush?

Activities

Jokes

Riddles are meant to tickle your funny bone and tease your friends. Try these on for size.

1. What do you find once in every minute, twice in every moment, and not once in a thousand years?

2. Mr. Green, the butcher, is forty years old, six feet tall, and wears size ten shoes. What do you think he weighs?

3. If your uncle's sister is not your aunt, who is she to you?

4. There were six fat ladies under one umbrella, but none got wet. Why?

5. What's the difference between an owl and a trumpet player?

Answers: 1. The letter M. 2. Meat, of course. 3. Your mother. 4. It wasn't raining. 5. One gives a hoot and the other gives a toot.

Make A Fireworks Picture

Fireworks can be safe and colorful when you follow this plan.

What You Need:

crayons	sheets of white drawing paper
black poster paint	scissors

What You Do:

- Choose colorful crayons, and cover a sheet of white paper with patches of different colors. Press firmly with the crayons to make a thick cover of color.
- Paint over the entire crayon-covered paper with black poster paint. Let it dry completely.
- With the edge of the scissors, gently scrape away the black paint to form a pattern or shape. Plan the pattern or shape before you begin.
- Try several fireworks pictures: a flag, a sunburst, a candle, a rocket.

Did You Know...?

You probably think all dogs can bark. But there is one that cannot. The Basenji is an African breed of hound dog that cannot bark. It can only whine. It's a small dog, weighing about 22 to 24 pounds. The tail of the Basenji is short and it forms a small circle. Most Basenji are brown and white with short silky hair.

There are volcanoes in outer space. Really. The biggest volcano we've discovered is 15 miles high—and it's not even on earth—it's on Mars!

You can find your way by following the stars. Sailors and wanderers have long used the stars for *navigating*, or finding their way. To figure out which way is north, look for the Big Dipper; then, follow the direction of the handle to spot the North Star.

Activities

Twinkle Star

Make your own twinkle stars and watch *your* stars come out every night.

What You Need:

newspaper	glue	glitter
a paper plate	pencil and scissors	yarn

What You Do:

- Spread out some newspaper to work on.
- Draw a large star in the center of the paper plate and cut it out.
- Dip the yarn in glue and outline the star with the yarn.
- Cover the whole star with the yarn. This is messy, but once the glitter is sprinkled on the gluey yarn, it'll be worth it.
- Sprinkle the glitter on the yarn and let it dry.
- Punch a hole through the yarn star and add a loop of yarn for hanging.
- Hang the star in your window and watch it glitter. Make a whole window full of stars!

Make A Map

What nationality are you? Find a map of the country of your nationality. Look in an *atlas* (a book of maps) or an encyclopedia. Trace or sketch a copy of the map. If your background is two or more nationalities, you can trace several maps or choose just one. After you have a copy on paper, you are ready to begin to make a salt and flour map. You may want to have an adult help you with this project.

What You Need:

a piece of cardboard
equal amounts of salt and
    flour (about 2 cups
    of each)

water
food coloring
paints
felt tip pens

newspaper
twigs
a bowl
paper cups

What You Do:

- Spread newspaper over your work area before you begin.
- Make an outline of your map on the cardboard, using the felt tip marker.
- Mix equal amounts of salt and flour. Add a small amount of water until you have a thick paste. You can color the paste by mixing in a few drops of food coloring. Put some of the paste in two or three paper cups, and color one blue for water, one green for grass, and one brown for earth.
- Spread the paste on the cardboard, keeping inside the map outline.
- Spread the paste about ½-inch thick. You can make a hill by mounding up some paste, but the thicker the mound, the longer it will take to dry. Let it dry for one or two days.
- On the dried map, you can use felt tip pens to draw roads, flowers, whatever you want on your map.

Variation:

If your country has lots of forests, you can add "trees" by using twigs from a real tree. Break the twigs into pieces one and two inches large. Stick each piece of twig into the map *before* it dries completely.

Activities

Trivia Game

Trivia are facts that may be unimportant but are very interesting. You can make up a game using trivia. Here are some to start you off. Put them on cards. Write the question on one side and the answer on the other. Stump your friends.

1. Q. Does hair grow faster at different times of day?
   A. Yes. Hair grows faster in the morning than any other time of day. Overall, hair grows about a half an inch a month.

2. Q. Which state has more lakes—Wisconsin or Florida?
   A. Florida, with about 30,000 lakes.

3. Q. What's the connection between grapefruit and grapes?
   A. Grapefruit gets its name because the fruit grows in bunches, just like grapes.